### Day Tripper Damian and the Aliens

Damian Crockett lives with his parents and younger sister, Bianca. They dote on Bianca, while despairing of their moody teenaged son. During a family outing Damian meets two aliens called Plingklopt and Plongklopt. Their spaceship is powered by laughter, so Damian asks a group of comedians to go back to Kloptronia with them telling jokes, in exchange for the gold the aliens can create from raw energy.

The aliens' little brother, Plug, has been accidentally left behind. With his neighbour, eleven year old Cressida Parker's help, Damian helps Plug to contact them and they arrange to meet in the local supermarket car park at midnight. It should have been simple but things do not go according to plan.

# Day Tripper Damian and the Aliens

Christine Price

ISBN 978-0-9561569-0-7

Cover design by Christine Price


Published 2009 by Christine Price
London SE14

Distribution at www.lulu.com

## ABOUT THE AUTHOR

CHRISTINE PRICE was born in Norfolk on the East coast of England. After studying to become a bi-lingual secretary, she moved to London where she began her career as an administrator in the wine trade. She then moved to the Communications Department of the Leprosy Mission. Following this, for many years she worked as PA to the Director of the development education charity, Worldaware, progressing to become the Co-ordinator of its Business Programme. For her work in promoting corporate social responsibility among British businesses, working in the developing world she was appointed MBE in 2003. After three years working at UCL Medical School, she is now working at the British Nutrition Foundation in London.

A lifelong Christian, Christine has used her communication skills in leading worship, teaching Bible studies and Sunday School classes and, more recently, organizing and leading writing workshops at her local church school.

# CHAPTER ONE

It was Bank Holiday Monday during that eerie twilight zone between the death of the Millennium Dome and the shining arrival of the $O_2$ Arena. Somewhere in South-East London Mrs. Crockett filled her lungs and bellowed up the stairs at a decibel level she hoped would overcome the house shaking thud of 'Scar Tissue' coming from her son's room.

"Damian! Turn that row off and come down here. We're all going out for the day."

Damian was disappointed that his new sound system, even at full volume, could not completely shut out his mother's voice. It rankled even more that his favourite band, 'Scar Tissue', who at their last gig had burst the eardrums of an unfortunate fan who had strayed too close to their mountainous banks of speakers, had failed to drown her out.

It was ten o'clock in the morning but Damian was still in his vest and underpants, neither of which had been parted from his body for several days. To avoid the inevitable nagging from his mother about the necessity to wash and change his clothes occasionally, Damian had perfected the art of creeping downstairs before dawn like some primitive hunter-gatherer to raid the kitchen for food. He would stockpile crisps, biscuits and boxes of cereals to be eaten dry or washed down with cola or, if he could get hold of it, his dad's beer.

The result was that his bedroom had become an indoor landfill site consisting of empty food packets, half-eaten snacks and sticky cans poking out between discarded clothes and single shoes. School books had been hurled bent and torn to distant corners of the room in the hope that they might conveniently self-destruct. More discreetly placed were the comic books which contained hidden inside them his secret stash of sexy lads' magazines.

There was, however, one bright spot in Damian's bedroom and it glowed with tender loving care. His new sound system, the ultimate product of Japanese micro-technology, could produce a sound equivalent to several jumbo jets while occupying a space no larger than a shoe box. It was treated with godlike reverence and was placed carefully on a crumpled copy of the Deptford Clarion to protect its precious feet. In the sound barrier war this was equivalent to the latest stealth bomber and yet still his mother's voice rose triumphant over her synthetic rival.

"Damian! Did you hear me? Turn that wretched machine off or I'll come up there right now and throw it out the window."

Damian knew that angry tone in his mother's voice and decided on a tactical withdrawal. With snail-like urgency he unwound himself from the duvet and reached out one weary arm to point his remote in the vague direction of the sound system. The silence was so sudden that for an instant Damian feared he had damaged his new best friend. He slithered off the bed and knelt before the shiny box with its perfectly matched twin speakers to make sure all was well. Satisfied he hauled himself back on to the bed and closed his eyes as if exhausted by the effort. However, the sound of Mrs. Crockett's footsteps on the stairs created an instantaneous burst of energy.

Damian leapt to his feet with his heart pounding, grabbing the nearest pair of dirt-stiffened jeans and his curry-stained black T-shirt. On no account must his mother see him semi-naked.

Mrs. Crockett opened the bedroom door purposefully but stopped on the threshold, her eyes and nose wrinkling in distaste at the sights and smells before her.

"Damian, it's like a pigsty in here. And why are you still wearing that filthy T-shirt when I brought up your clean things yesterday?" Before he could control his eyes they flicked towards a tumbled pile of rags in the corner which only a few hours before had been a neat pile of ironing. He braced himself for the tirade as her eyes followed his to their target.

"Damian, I spent hours doing that ironing," screamed Mrs. Crockett, almost crying with frustration. "You keep going on at me that you want to be treated like an adult but it's like having a baby in the house again. I know being a teenager isn't easy. They're always going on about it on the telly. But I just don't know what to do with you. If your little sister can manage to wash and keep herself tidy, why can't you?"

Damian had hardened himself against these regular and unwelcome comparisons to his sister, Bianca. She had been a late and unexpected addition to the family and, as such, was doted on by her parents. Now at seven years old she was cute and manipulative enough to have them grovelling adoringly at her feet. Only he, Damian, had been clever enough to see through her and because of it had earned many a humiliation at her hands. She could not fool him; she could not get round him. Like a cat rubbing round his legs she had tried to make him adore her like everyone else did, but he would have none of it. The more she smiled and pleaded to be loved, the more he knew she was a witch in disguise and he would prove it one day.

"Damian, are you listening to me?" His mother's voice cut across his murderous thoughts.

"Yeah." The solitary word came mumbling out like toothpaste being squeezed reluctantly out of its tube.

Mrs. Crockett stuck her hands on her hips with grim determination. "Just for once your father and I want to go out for the day like any normal family. Will you please have a wash, put on some clean clothes and get downstairs."

"OK." Although the response was compliant, Mrs. Crockett saw no evidence of accompanying action, so she gave up and turned away, muttering to herself.

\* \* \*

Damian slouched down the stairs trying to look moody and bored, mimicking his hero, Zitmeister, lead singer with Scar Tissue. He had waved a flannel in the direction of his face and dug out some cleanish-looking underwear. He would have liked to go commando but previous experience had taught him that the level of discomfort seriously undermined his desire to be macho. The jeans were the same but the offending black T-shirt had been replaced with a dingy grey one which bore the legend "Don't push me!" Only at ground level was dirt conspicuous by its absence. Damian's mother had almost fainted when she saw the price of the trainers her son had pleaded with her to buy because all his mates were wearing them and he'd look a nerd in anything else. To her mind they made his feet look twice their normal size but she had eventually given in. Damian cherished them because they had the right logo to keep him in with his peers.

Mr. & Mrs Crockett and Bianca were waiting in the hallway. Mrs Crockett was fussing over girly pink hair ties in Bianca's blonde curls. The little girl spotted Damian on the stairs and pounced, "Damian's got gunk on his hair." All eyes zeroed in on Damian and he felt the aura of cool slipping away and self-consciousness taking its place. He inwardly cursed the way his already embarrassing sticky-out ears reddened and burned.

"Damian, what have you done to yourself?" Mrs. Crockett grabbed her son by the arm and held him in a surprisingly strong grip while she swatted at the tangled tufts of gel-laden hair. Damian tried to fend her off with his free hand but the carefully sculptured spikes he

5

had created were unceremoniously flattened. The hair now clung to his scalp like an old-fashioned bathing hat.

"Aw Mum," he grunted knowing that further resistance was futile. Bianca smiled in that knowingly innocent way of hers and Damian silently swore revenge.

Mr. Crockett looked at his son with ill-disguised bewilderment. He couldn't understand where the friendly, affectionate boy he'd played football with not that long ago had gone. They had been best mates then, now he just felt like a cash machine who had to use what little spare money he had to bribe and cajole this sullen stranger who now occupied his son's room.

"Let's get a move on otherwise there'll be no point in going at all."

* * *

Mrs. Crockett liked to sit next to her husband in the car so that she could help him navigate. The fact that she had no conception of left and right, nor could she read road signs until they were level with the car seemed to her no impediment at all. She would cheerily shout 'turn left' while flinging her right arm dangerously into her husband's face. Mr. Crockett had, over the years, realised that his wife's hands were a far better indicator of the correct route than her mouth and so would turn in the direction of whatever set of fingers waggled furiously against the windscreen. For the most part, however, he was content in the knowledge that he was a Londoner born and bred and could, therefore, find his way around without any help at all, provided those idiots at the Council stopped mucking about with their wretched gyratory systems and traffic calming exercises.

This harmonious set up in the front of the car meant that by necessity Damian had to sit in the back with Bianca. Such a fate was not only incredibly uncool but fraught with danger. With both parents momentarily looking elsewhere Bianca would often display the devilish horns which lurked underneath her usual angelic halo.

"Do you know where we're going Damian?" she asked sweetly.

"Poxy Greenwich by the look of it," grunted Damian.

Bianca pursed her lips in mock exasperation, "Actually, we're going to the Party Pod and Daddy said I'd got such a good report from my teacher that I could go on any of the rides I liked, so there."

Damian groaned. Not the Party Pod. Some bright spark had thought it would be a great idea to use the empty Millennium Dome as a temporary eco-friendly greenhouse – London's answer to the Eden Project. The developers stuck in a few endangered trees and plants to rubberstamp their green credentials and then proceeded to get their hands on lots of government conservation grants. The rest of the space was filled with the cheapest, tackiest funfair rides they could find, interspersed with overpriced junk food outlets. An expensive all-day car park completed the picture of environmental heaven.

To Damian it was the pits. He clamped the headphones of his iPod firmly over his ears and pulled the baseball cap he'd hurriedly clamped over his flattened hair well down over his eyes to blot out the awfulness of the situation. Slumping as low down in the car seat as possible, he prayed that none of his mates would see him.

# CHAPTER TWO

The doors of the pressurised airlock gave a self-important swoosh as they opened to allow the next group of visitors into the Pod. Hundreds of interlocking panes of tinted super-glass had been put in to form an artificial sky of soft blue over their heads; its perfection only spoiled by the flocks of pigeons which roosted on the outside. Damian wondered idly whether eventually the weight of droppings would make the roof cave in, killing everyone below. Perhaps he could make his fortune selling the film rights to Hollywood – 'Drop Zone - Attack of the Killer Pigeons'. He could get Scar Tissue to do the music and grab a percentage of the merchandising rights on stuffed pigeons which dropped sticky white pellets from their rear end.

"Mummy look! Can I go on the lily pond?" Bianca's excited voice tried to make itself heard over the shouts and giggles of thousands of children clambering over the rides like locusts in a wheat field. Mr. Crockett began to think that a Bank Holiday wasn't the best day to come.

"We'll see, dear," smiled Mrs. Crockett. She and Bianca headed towards a giant lime green plastic frog sitting in the middle of a large artificial pond. Around its head small metal flies on wires circled endlessly and every 15 minutes precisely the frog's red plastic tongue darted out to grab one into its deep hollow mouth; only for it to reappear again a few seconds later to join the swarm once more.

Surrounding the frog on the hardboard pond were giant fibreglass lilies on wheels inside of which small children bobbed about, delightedly twirling the big flowers around so that they knocked into each other with loud crunching noises. Mrs. Crockett looked doubtful as to the safety of this arrangement but gave in to Bianca's pleading. She watched anxiously as Bianca flung herself from side to side in order to hit as many other lilies as possible. One child foolishly gripped the sides of his lily with his fingers and Bianca seemed to take fiendish delight in crashing heavily into him. Damian thought the boy's resulting screams might indeed bring down the glass roof, but no such luck. Mr. & Mrs. Crockett rushed over to placate both child and angry parent.

Damian saw his chance of escape and wandered away looking nonchalant. He couldn't go out of the main exit because the bar code on his ticket would be cancelled when he used it to open the airlock. He needed to be able to get back in so that in a couple of hours, when his parents tired of indulging Bianca, he could reappear as if by magic and claim to have been having a great time in the ecological section.

Wandering slowly round the hermetically-sealed perimeter trying not to look conspicuous, Damian searched for a way out. Eventually he spotted a small air vent hidden behind some droopy-looking palm trees. It was easy enough to remove the mesh cover and he started to crawl through. The vent was corrugated like a large, silver washing machine hose and scrunched like bubble wrap under his knees.

10

Suddenly Damian saw two shadows bouncing off the tubular wall ahead of him from around the next bend. He took off his headphones and listened. The slap, slap, of bodies moving along the plastic was unmistakable. Someone was trying to sneak in to the Pod while he was trying to sneak out. Just as he was wondering what to do, two faces appeared in the grey gloom which penetrated the tunnel. But these were no ordinary faces, each had three enormous purple eyes which filled the bottom of the face. Above them were three sets of lips – small, medium and large. The head was bright green with glowing filaments, like those on a fibre-optic lamp, forming a collar round the neck.

The bodies on which these strange heads rested appeared, by contrast, oddly ordinary. They were about the size of a small child and were dressed in matching cotton shirts and dungarees, with toddlers' pale blue mittens and multi-coloured Wellingtons.

Damian didn't know whether to laugh or scream but, before he could do either, one of the creatures spoke, through its middle mouth, in the kind of posh English only associated with royalty.

"Excuse us, we've just come down from Newcastle-upon-Tyne for the day and seem to have got lost. Could you direct us to the entrance of the Party Pod?

Now even though Damian had never been out of London and, despite the fact that his dad had told him that all Northerners were strange, he knew for a fact that these two were not from Newcastle – nor anywhere else on the planet.

"Pull the other one, mate," he said.

The two creatures looked at each other, six eyes dancing around in bewilderment. "Pull the other what?" they said in unison.

"You know, 'pull the other leg', it's an expression innit. Means you're telling porkies."

"No, no, we are not the animals you call pigs, we are humans and we wish to visit the Party Pod, please."

Damian tried again. "Now look, I don't know who or what you are, but you certainly ain't human. What you doin' 'ere?"

"We assure you, we are human and not the porky pigs."

Damian moved closer to them so that they could see him clearly. "Come off it. This," he said, pointing to his own grubby features, "is a human face. What do you call that?" He jabbed dramatically at one of the green heads but quickly pulled his finger away when he realised it now had an oily green glow.

The two creatures started jabbering away to each other, using the smallest of their mouths, in a language which consisted of whistles and squeaks. Seemingly reaching some sort of agreement, they nodded to each other and turned to face Damian.

"My name is Plingklopt and this is my sister, Plongklopt. If it's easier you can call us Pling and Plong."

"Wow! So you're really extra terrestrials – wicked. My name's Damian, pleased to meet you." Damian shook each mittened hand in turn while mentally planning how he would impress his mates with this close encounter of the alien kind.

"We are from the planet Kloptronia."

Damian wasn't sure whether it was Pling or Plong speaking because they were identical but it didn't matter as both were equally cool. "What you doin' in Greenwich then?"

"We've been stranded on earth and we need help to get back to Kloptronia."

"Say no more," replied Damian, "I'm your man. You just tell me what the problem is and I'll sort it out."

The Kloptronians seemed rather puzzled by Damian's particular version of the English language, but nodded anyway.

Pling began to explain. "Energy on our planet is created by harnessing the positive emotions of the inhabitants. When we laugh, using our biggest mouth, that laughter is converted into the power we need to run our systems – rather like your electricity. So, the more we laugh, the more power we have and we can use it to synthesize anything – including our food. It means everything is recycled. Laughing gives us energy, energy gives us food, which gives us energy to laugh. Do you understand?"

"Yeah, but which mouth do you eat with?"

"Oh all of them, Kloptronians love to eat."

"But do you have to, you know, go to the toilet like us humans?"

Damian thought he detected a darkening of their green skin, which he took to be a sort of blush. Plong answered, "No, not in the way you mean. But occasionally, if we eat too much and produce surplus energy, it comes out in a huge burp." She put a mittened hand over her mouths and tinkled like a little bell, presumably in embarrassment.

"So, why come to Greenwich?" asked Damian.

"Well," said Pling, "we were on a mission to chart a new black hole near your solar system when an asteroid storm blew us off course and we landed here. Your little planet is several thousand light years away from Kloptronia and we don't have enough power to get back."

Damian was a bit put out to have his home described as a 'little planet' and replied rather sharply, "Not so much of the 'little' if you don't mind. We're very proud of our world."

"From what we have seen over the last couple of days this pride of yours seems to consist of doing the best you can to use up your world's resources as quickly as possible without replacing them, and leaving as much mess and destruction behind as you can."

Damian looked a bit crestfallen. "All right, nuff said. But it ain't my fault, it's the leaders, innit."

"Oh? Wasn't it you we saw in the car park a little while ago throwing his half-chewed bubble gum on to the ground and walking away?"

"Yeah well, let's get back to your problem, shall we? I'm not the one who needs help." Pling and Plong gave each other meaningful looks with all six of their eyes as if to show that they weren't too sure about that.

As Plong started to speak again Damian thought he detected globs of green goo forming around her eyes. "The problem is that we're so miserable and scared here that we can't laugh. We just want to cry all the time." A large blob of the goo slithered from her face on to the floor of the tunnel. Pling patted her arm and went on, "And, even if we laughed ourselves silly for months, we still couldn't produce enough power by ourselves to get all the way back to Kloptronia."

"That's bad," said Damian, "What can I do to help?"

"Well, we thought if we could get inside the Party Pod where all those human children are laughing, we could harness their energy to get us home." said Pling.

"I see. But won't human energy gum up the works?"

"Normally, yes," said Plong, "but we've managed to make this adaptor unit to filter out the harmful bits." From behind her in the tunnel Plong pulled a small knapsack from which she brought out what looked like a large fishing net with a handle. From the bottom of the net a tube was connected to a crystal nestling inside the bag. "All we have to do is wave this around among the children to capture the laughter and the Kloptronian crystal will do the rest." All three of her mouths smiled at the mastery of this plan.

Damian stroked his chin thoughtfully. "I think you might have a problem there," he said.

"Why?" they both asked surprised.

"Down here on earth people are a bit iffy about aliens, if you know what I mean. We expect them to want to conquer the world and kill everybody, stuff like that. If you go wandering round looking like that amongst all those kids you'll get arrested, or taken for experimentation, or exterminated or something."

"Aren't these human costumes sufficient disguise? We chose them very carefully to fit in."

16

"No, they ain't. We don't have many children here with three eyes and three mouths, you know. By the way, how do you hear and smell things?"

"Oh, the fibres round our neck detect sound and smell."

"What? Those wavy things do both? We have ears to hear with and a nose to smell with," said Damian, pointing out the relevant parts.

Plong looked unimpressed. "You can't see sounds and you can't see smells, they're both invisible. So why should you need two different detectors?"

"The point is we do, so let's not go on about it, OK?" Damian didn't like the suggestion that humans might be inferior.

Pling tried to sooth him. "We don't mean any harm, honestly. We had enough energy to change our bodies but not our heads. Will people really notice?"

Damian nodded very slowly and very deliberately as if to emphasise the point. "Perhaps if I go and speak to them first and explain that you're only borrowing the laughter…" Damian didn't get to finish the sentence.

"Excuse me, Mr Damian, but I'm afraid we have to take the laughter permanently. We didn't think it would matter because you

17

earthlings seem to like being miserable all the time." Plong looked apologetic.

"Oh, so now you're saying you're going to nick all our laughter and leave us permanently depressed. Thanks a lot. I really ought to hand you over to the police or something. You're nutters" Even while he uttered this threat Damian knew very well he had no intention of sharing his 'first contact' with anyone.

"Do you really think the people in the Pod would be upset?" asked Pling.

"Upset? That's not the half of it, mate. It would be the extermination chamber for you, for definite."

"What do you think we should do then?" Pling was beginning to go a darker shade of green again in agitation at the thought of being exterminated.

Damian thought for a moment and scratched his head under the baseball cap. Then a notice his dad had pointed out as they entered the car park prised itself out of his memory. He had an idea. "Tell me," he asked, "can the power you generate be used to create anything you like?"

"Yes, provided we know the molecular structure and we have enough energy."

"Good," said Damian. "Follow me."

* * *

Damian sneaked back into the Pod and 'borrowed' two hoodies from a couple of children who were too busy flicking organic paint at each other in the Creative Zone to notice. They were a bit big for Pling and Plong but the hoods did the job of covering their heads. Damian only hoped that the sight of two apparently young people with their hoods up on a bright, sunny day wouldn't get the security staff all steamed up about hooligans and muggers on the prowl. He led the way across the car park, trying to avoid the CCTV cameras. A second, smaller Pod nestled in the shadow of its bigger brother. The sign at the entrance proclaimed 'Performance Pod – continuous entertainment - a different show every hour (also bookable for private functions, call 0800 34567)'. The door was not a hi-tech airlock like the main Pod but a turnstile with a bored-looking 'Visitor Assistant' sitting reading the paper.

"Next show's not for half an hour," she muttered, not raising her eyes from the day's headlines.

"But the notice says 'continuous entertainment'," said Damian.

The woman dragged her eyes reluctantly from the newspaper and gave him one of those withering looks which adults reserve for children who are being particularly stupid and/or difficult. Damian took the hint and moved away.

Once out of sight, Damian quickly dragged the Kloptronians round to the back of the Pod where there was a tatty notice which said 'Performers' Entrance'. An ill-fitting tarpaulin served as a door and, as there were thankfully no security staff around, Damian led the way inside. The interior was gloomy and smelled of damp. Pling and Plong wanted to leave because it was sapping their energy, but Damian urged them on. He could hear voices beyond a small partitioned area to his left. Stuck on the outside was a well-used poster:

*The Stand-Up Show (as seen on TV)*

*All Your Favourite Comedians reunited for one unforgettable nationwide tour*

*Barbara Blagg, Seamus O'Murphy, Eddie Bernstein, Polly Tickle-Correctness and starring the dynamic duo - Supercomic and Chuckle Boy*

Damian had never actually seen any of these people because the show had been on television before he was born, but his dad had been a devoted fan and invariably bemoaned their loss whenever some 'new-fangled tosh' dared to invade his screen. 'Call that humour, he'd say, 'squeezing blackheads is more entertaining than that. The Stand-up Show, now that was funny.' A nostalgic mist would settle over his eyes, though when pressed he could never remember any of the jokes.

Peering gingerly round the edge of the partition, the sight which greeted Damian's expectant eyes made him doubt the wisdom of his plan, but it was too late to go back now.

"'Scuse me, mate, are you the stand-up comedians from the telly?"

A surly-looking man with a jet black wig which flicked up at the neck, allowing wisps of grey hair to escape from underneath, managed a curt response. "Who wants to know?"

"My name's Damian and my dad thinks you're the greatest. Can we get your autographs?" Keeping their hoods well down over their faces, Damien led Pling and Plong into the make-shift dressing room.

The man with the wig turned out to be Eddie Bernstein and he introduced his fellow comedians while Damian dug out a scrappy piece of paper he'd torn from his geography book several days earlier in order to prevent his teacher from seeing that he'd placed Calcutta in the middle of Kansas. Barbara Blagg was tall and skinny and bent to peer into Damian's face like a curious giraffe. Seamus O'Murphy was dressed up like a leprechaun and wore large plastic pointed ears which were cracked with age. His once magnificent red beard was now completely grey and frizzled. Damian looked around for Polly Tickle-Correctness - his dad had said she was an absolute stunner and he wouldn't have minded giving her a few one-liners. But the years had not been kind to her and, when a dyed-blonde whale of a woman waddled over and said, "Hi, I'm Polly" and batted her false eyelashes at him, Damian smiled nervously and took a step backwards.

A high squeaky voice from the corner caught his attention. "Aren't you going to introduce us, Eddie?" Eddie made an extravagant theatrical bow and bellowed, "Ladies and gentlemen, may I introduce to you the world-famous Supercomic and Chuckle Boy." A small, dapper middle-aged man waltzed from the corner in the exaggerated, hip-swaying way of a super model. "Helloooo, I'm Supercomic, but you can call me Eugene. And this is my partner Chuckle Boy – or Gus as he's known." Eugene waved a rather limp hand in the direction of a short, stocky man with several days' growth of beard and a cigarette hanging out of his mouth.

"Your friends don't say very much, do they." Barbara was craning her skinny neck towards Pling and Plong who were hovering near the door.

"Oh, they're shy," said Damian nervously.

"Come on, let's have a look at them." Before Damian could stop her she had pulled back their hoods and a bloodcurdling scream had left her throat. Damian quickly stepped between her and the aliens and tried to retrieve the situation.

"It's all right, they're really very friendly. They won't hurt you, I promise."

Everyone eyed Pling and Plong suspiciously, while keeping a safe distance. Eddie broke the awkward silence. "What are they? Circus freaks or something?"

"No," answered Damian. "They're extra terrestrials from the planet Kloptronia and they need your help."

"Don't be ridiculous," said Eugene, "There's no such thing. It's just a good make-up job." He went over to Pling and ran his finger down the alien's face to see whether the green would come off.

"Please don't do that," said Pling curtly in his posh voice. Eugene jumped back abruptly at the sound of his plummy tones. "We *are* aliens and we *are* from the planet Kloptronia."

"Perhaps we could give them a spot in the show," offered Polly. "They are rather cute." There were murmurs of approval at this suggestion.

"No, that's not what they need. You have to travel back to Kloptronia with them," said Damian triumphantly.

A collective gasp went round the room. "Why on earth would we want to do that?" asked Seamus.

"Because when you get there my friends will pay you with as much gold as you can carry."

Plong whispered in Damian's ear, "What's gold?"

Damian hissed back, "It's a metal that's very valuable on earth." Just then he noticed the rather flashy medallion Eugene was wearing round his neck. He pointed. "That's gold. You wouldn't have any problem making that, would you?" Plong went to examine the medallion and a soft yellow light shone from one of her eyes on to the surface.

Eugene looked uncomfortable. "It's not exactly pure gold, you know."

Plong looked up and said, "I've isolated the 10% of pure metal you call gold. It would be very easy to synthesise. In fact, I'm surprised you value it so highly." Damian glowered at her and mouthed 'shut up'.

Eddie was a bit dubious. "How do we know you really can make gold?"

"Would you like me to show you?" asked Plong. She took out the crystal from her knapsack and the yellow light from her eye played down on it. A moment later a nugget of gold the size of a walnut appeared in her hand. Everyone gasped and huddled round to have a closer look.

Gus, who had left his perch in the corner, eyed the nugget greedily. "Why don't we just keep the little fellahs here and make them produce gold for us?"

Damian answered quickly before this idea had time to take root. "That wouldn't work. The reason you have to go to Kloptronia with them is that they need laughter to generate the power to make things like gold. Since being on earth they've used up nearly all their energy so they need to get back to Kloptronia to recharge their batteries."

"Pity," muttered Gus and sloped back to the corner.

"How long would this trip take?" asked Eddie, "We are in the middle of a nationwide tour, you know."

"If all of you came, it would take about six of your earth months," said Pling.

"Six months," cried Eugene in a tortured voice. "I can't possibly do without seeing my lifestyle consultant for six months."

"For a sackful of gold I'd do without air for six months," muttered Seamus.

"What do we have to do to get this gold?" asked Barbara suspiciously. "I don't fancy being poked and prodded about like a lab rat."

"Oh I don't know, it might be quite nice to be poked and prodded again," sighed Polly.

"It's quite simple," said Damien, "you just have to do what you always do - tell jokes."

"What?" They all said together.

"Every time you tell a joke which makes Plong and Pling laugh, it helps them fuel their space ship. If you all join in and laugh as well, the ship will go even faster and you'll be back quicker."

"Sounds daft to me," said Seamus, "whoever heard of a space ship running on laughter."

"Let me demonstrate," said Damian. Looking at the two aliens he began, "My dog has no nose."

Being hardened professionals the comedians all immediately piped up with "How does it smell?"

"Bloomin' awful," finished Damien.

The effect on Plong and Pling was instantaneous. Their three eyes started to crinkle up, the antenna round their necks glowed all the colours of the rainbow and their three mouths produced a honking sound like a flock of geese. The Kloptronian crystal began to glow brightly and gradually the aliens rose from the floor and began to bob about on the ceiling.

"How can they laugh at that crummy old joke?" asked Seamus.

"Simple," said Damien, "They've never heard it before."

# CHAPTER THREE

Without committing themselves to the trip, the comedians did agree to take a look at the Kloptronian spaceship. As the aliens led the way across the car park the entertainers bickered between themselves as to what to do for the best. Being the star, Eugene had the most misgivings.

"We're supposed to be professionals and I think we should honour our contract and finish all the tour dates here before we go wandering off into outer space. My fans all around the country are expecting to see me and I don't think I should disappoint them."

"Come off it," said Eddie, "you haven't had any fans for years. Just look at the audiences we've had at the Performance Pod this past week – a couple of drunks, a group from the old people's home who fell asleep and a stray dog."

"But it will be different once we get out of London," wailed Eugene, unwilling to acknowledge his fall from fame.

"Yeah," interrupted Barbara, "even the dogs won't come." Everyone laughed and they had to stop Pling and Plong from becoming airborne again.

"I tell you what," said Eddie taking out his mobile phone, "I'll ring Lew and ask his opinion."

While they all waited expectantly, Eddie dialled the number of their agent, Lew Goldenstein, and started jabbering away to the disembodied voice at the end of the phone. With a decisive snap he switched off the mobile and delivered the verdict.

"Lew says advance bookings for the rest of the tour are so bad that some venues are ringing to cancel. He also says if we have the opportunity to get six months' paid work, we should go for it – remembering his ten per cent, of course."

"Well, I guess that's it then," said Barbara, "Kloptronia here we come."

"Who knows, perhaps we can use our experiences in the act when we get back," added Polly.

"I for one am never being Chuckle Boy ever again once I've got my hands on the gold," said Gus, at which remark Eugene looked as if he might burst into tears. Gus squeezed his hand affectionately saying, "Don't worry, old girl, I'll be your personal manager and lifestyle consultant all in one."

Pling and Plong stopped in front of an old transit van. "This is it," they said.

The others looked worried. "What's going on? This isn't some joke is it? You haven't got hidden TV cameras watching us make complete fools of ourselves believing in aliens?"

"No, it's all right," said Pling reassuringly. "We had to disguise the ship so that it wouldn't be seen. We just transformed it into this van so that it would fit in with all the other shabby vehicles in the car park." The fact that the van was parked next to his dad's rather old hatchback made Damian blush. "Just wait a moment," said Pling.

The aliens turned the yellow beams from their eyes on to the van and it dissolved and reformed into a large silver globe which hovered just above the ground. A hatchway opened up in the side with steps to the ground and they all clambered on board.

Inside the ship nothing seemed to be real or solid. Walls faded in and out of view, instrument consoles kept appearing and disappearing on different sides of the cabin. The comedians looked worried.

"Where will we sleep?" they asked. "And what will we eat?"

Plong answered, "Once you start telling us jokes and the ship powers up properly, you can decide exactly what sort of rooms you'd like and they will form themselves for you."

"And," added Pling, "any sort of food you'd like will just appear in your hand."

"This sounds like heaven," sighed Polly.

Plong consulted some panels in front of her and looked anxious. "We ought to get going. Our energy levels are dangerously low. Could you start telling some jokes, please?"

And so the flood of old jokes began – chickens crossing roads, endless 'knock knocks', non-politically correct stories about Scotsmen, Irishmen and Englishmen and, of course, mothers-in-law. The aliens began honking with delight and the ship began to hum contentedly.

"Wait," shouted Damien, "You've got to let me out first."

"Don't you want to come with us Mr. Damian?" asked Pling.

"Yeah, of course I would" he said sadly, "but my parents wouldn't like it if I just disappeared for six months without a word. They drive me mad, but I wouldn't want to upset them that much."

Green goo started to appear in all six of Pling's and Plong's eyes. They hugged Damien and several large dollops landed on his T-shirt. Reluctantly they gave him back the two hooded jackets to return to their rightful owners and let Damien make his way down the ladder to the car park. They were about to close the hatch when Damien remembered something. He pulled out the scrappy piece of paper from his geography book and a biro with the end broken off. Scribbling quickly he ran up the steps and pressed the paper into Pling's hand.

"It's got my address on it. When you bring the others back, don't forget to look me up."

"We won't," they called and the hatch slowly closed in front of them.

Damien stood watching as the silver globe started to turn pale white and then disappear completely leaving no trace. He felt something in his jeans' pocket, it was the gold nugget.

Just then he heard a bored, lifeless voice echo across the car park from the address system. "Would customers please note that the Party Pod will be closing in precisely 15 minutes. We hope you have enjoyed your visit. Come again soon." Good grief, thought Damien, I'd better get back in there fast.

He hurried back to the air vent and crawled out from behind the palm trees, dumping the two sweatshirts in the plant pot. The crowds were much thinner now so his family were easy to spot. His mum and dad were dragging Bianca away from a stand selling imitation jungle insects made out of chocolate and for some inexplicable reason she was clutching a rather ugly garden gnome.

"Bianca, you're not having anything else to eat. You've already embarrassed us enough today throwing up over that nice little boy just because he wanted to hold your hand on the snake ride." It was the first time Damian had ever heard his mother's angry voice directed at his little sister.

"Mother, I think we've spoiled that girl," added his father with annoyance.

Damien began to think that maybe, just maybe, Bianca's starring role in the Crockett household might just be coming to an end. A slow smile began to spread over his face, but then he noticed something on Bianca's dress and his triumph turned to horror. There on the hem was a small blob of green goo, just like the stains on his T-shirt.

His mind began turning somersaults, trying to make sense of it. Had she managed to get away from their parents in order to follow him to the space ship? Had Plong and Pling lied to him? Were there other Kloptronians in the Pod that day, all trying to steal human laughter? But worst of all came the realisation that perhaps Bianca was not what she seemed. Had he been living with an alien all this time without knowing it? He had to find out and in order to do so he would have to play the part she had always wanted - adoring big brother. The thought made him feel sick, but he smiled engagingly at this parents and said, "It's not Bianca's fault she's sick, she's always been delicate, you know that."

"That's true," they said, somewhat surprised at his concern for his sister. "Anyway, where have you been all this time?"

"Oh just mooching around," said Damian.

Bianca chose just that moment to throw up once more all over Damian's precious trainers. But he just smiled through gritted teeth and said, "Oh you poor thing, here let me carry that beautiful gnome for you. Did you win it? You're so clever."

And so the game was on but he was determined to be the winner.

# CHAPTER FOUR

Normally on a school day breakfast in the Crockett household was a noisy affair, but this morning was different. Despite her protestations and pleadings Bianca had been sent to bed the previous evening as soon as the family got home from the Party Pod. She had spent a restless night feeling both aggrieved at being treated so shamefully by her parents and uncertain as to how to restore herself to her rightful position as queen of the house. In the end she had decided to mount a silent protest, getting herself ready for school and eating her breakfast without a word, while every so often gazing with pained, tear-reddened eyes at her mother and sighing dramatically.

Mrs Crockett was unsure how to deal with this behaviour. Part of her knew it was all an act and that she should ignore it. On the other hand, this was her baby, and the temptation to hug the child and plead for forgiveness in the face of those accusing blue eyes was overwhelming. For once it was Mr Crocket who took the initiative, putting down the newspaper which he invariably used as a barrier to protect himself form his quarrelsome family.

"Bianca will you please stop that dreadful sighing. It's putting me off my breakfast."

Bianca pouted extravagantly and folded her arms to show her displeasure.

"And you needn't look at me like that, young lady," added Mr Crockett frowning. "You acted like a spoiled brat at the Party Pod yesterday and it seems sending you to bed early was not sufficient punishment to improve your behaviour this morning. Mother, I think Bianca should spend every evening at home this week…"

Before he could finish Bianca stood up from the table with her fists clenched tight as if she were about to explode with rage.

"…and there'll be no watching DVDs in her bedroom either. She can sit downstairs with us."

Mrs Crockett seemed stunned by this show of parental authority from her husband. "Well, if you say so dear. But it's the parents' evening at Bianca's ballet class this evening and she's doing a solo. We wouldn't want to miss that, would we?"

Mr Crockett looked annoyed at having his perfect plan questioned. "Well, why didn't you tell me? No one ever tells me anything in this house. I've arranged for the garden centre to deliver a load of bedding plants and fertiliser this evening. I've got to be here to help move them into the back garden."

"Actually, dear, I told you three weeks ago and put it on the calendar and in your office diary," said Mrs Crockett, looking hurt. "I can't help it if you've arranged a delivery without checking first."

Mr Crockett could see he had been outmanoeuvred by this small oversight on his part. Why should he think to check if they'd be going out in the evening; they never went out in the evening.

For Damian too this school day was different. It usually took several increasingly desperate cries from his mother before he would get up at the last minute and rush out of the front door with little more than a grunt of greeting to his family. This morning, however, he was on a mission and so had actually responded to the first call of his alarm clock in order to be ready to join them for a leisurely breakfast. Damian smiled to himself and considered the effort well worth it as he watched with relish the unfolding drama over Bianca. Now was his chance.

"Dad, you and Mum mustn't miss Bianca's starring role. I'll stay here and help the delivery man move everything into the back garden."

Mr and Mrs Crockett and Bianca all eyed Damian with a certain degree of suspicion and disbelief, so he thought he'd better couch his offer in slightly more believable terms. "It'll only cost you ten quid," he grinned.

"Oh all right," sighed Mr Crockett, "but you're only getting a fiver. There aren't *that* many plants and I'm not *that* desperate to see a children's ballet."

"Deal," said Damian, inwardly congratulating himself for arranging to have the house to himself that evening. He could search

Bianca's room for clues about where the green goo on her dress had come from *and* make some money as well.

"Daddy, can I have five pounds if I do my dance nicely?" said Bianca, putting on her sweetest, most dazzling smile.

To Damian it seemed that his dad clutched his newspaper just a little bit more tightly as he got up to leave for work. He could tell the urge to swat Bianca was very hard to resist. Mrs Crockett noticed it too and quickly intervened.

"I think you should thank your father for allowing you to dance at all this evening," she said sternly.

Bianca took the hint, gritted her teeth, and mumbled, "Thank you, Daddy."

* * *

Damian was convinced there was a government conspiracy to make all the clocks in every school in the country go at half normal speed. Normally, this would only be a minor irritation, as he had mastered the art of filling the time by replaying his favourite 'Scar Tissue' tracks in his head, like a human iPod. Today he couldn't even concentrate on 'Scar Tissue', so his teachers had no chance of capturing his attention for even the briefest of moments to impart a few grains of knowledge. All Damian could think about was getting the day over so that he could begin his investigation into Bianca's room.

38

As soon as the final bell went Damian was out of the classroom and through the main doors before his long-suffering form teacher could even draw breath to speak. His gaggle of mates were equally astonished to see him *run* down the road to catch the first bus home. Usually a slow amble was called for, so that the girls could see how cool they all were. The idea was to walk towards the bus just slowly enough to irritate the driver but not so slowly that he actually had time to close the doors and leave them behind. He, and everyone else, had to be made aware that this was their personal conveyance, to be used in their own time, and not lowly public transport.

Damian had no time for such games today. He had to get to Bianca's room. In fact he was in such a hurry to get through the front door that he almost broke his key in the lock.

"Damian, be careful, you nearly knocked me over!" His mother was just behind the front door putting her coat on.

Damian had been so sure the house would be empty that he almost fainted with the shock of finding his mother there. He had to recover himself quickly. "Er, sorry mum. I thought you'd have gone to collect Bianca from school by now."

"I'm just on my way now. It's you that's early. Normally you come strolling in long after this. What's your rush?" Mrs Crockett asked suspiciously.

Damian thought quickly, "Oh I, er, just wanted to be here, you know, in time for the, er, delivery people."

"Strange how you can always shift yourself when money's involved," said Mrs. Crockett tartly. "Oh well, at least you're here. We'll see you after the performance – around 6.30 I should think." As she walked through the front door Mrs. Crockett called over her shoulder, "There's some salad in the fridge if you're hungry."

"Don't worry, mum, I'll probably get some chips once the plants have arrived."

Damian could hear his mother muttering to herself as she walked down the path, "Chips, that's all they ever want to eat. I don't know why I bother trailing round the supermarket for food. I might just as well take out a season ticket at the chippie."

He started to run up the stairs and had got half way when he remembered that his mother had recently had a new stair carpet laid and there was now a 'pain of death' embargo on anyone going upstairs with their shoes on. He sat down on the nearest step and pulled off his school shoes, tossing them down to the foot of the stairs to land in a heap by the coat rack. So far his mother had turned a blind eye to him keeping his beloved trainers in his bedroom because they were a match for any new carpet in terms of cleanliness. However, he did not wish to lose this concession, especially as it had taken him ages to get

Bianca's sick off the trainers and restored them to near perfect condition.

Damian quickly threw off the rest of his school uniform, gathering up the bits to throw in a heap in the corner. He then pulled on his oldest, tattiest jeans and started searching round for a suitably disgusting T shirt to go with them. An evil smile sneaked across his face as he noticed the brand-new, cellophane wrapped packet on top of his wardrobe. Bianca had bought him a pale orange T shirt with a large picture of a teddy bear dressed as a punk rocker on the front for Christmas. While thanking her sweetly in front of his parents, inwardly he had sworn never to wear it and had tossed the offending garment unopened as far out of sight as he could. Now it would be perfect for his covert expedition into Bianca's room as it smelled of newness rather than Damian. As a further stroke of genius he was sure that when the plants arrived he could arrange for a large rip and/or stain to render it fit for nothing but the dustbin.

* * *

Damian had washed his hands and feet more carefully than he had ever done in his life and had sprayed himself liberally with his father's deodorant. The new carpet tickled his toes as he crept towards Bianca's bedroom door. He knew it was silly to creep about when the house was empty but it all added to the feeling of adventure. He almost wished he could wear a balaclava or rub dirt on his face like the SAS did in the movies.

On her door was a china plaque in the shape of a pink fairy with 'Bianca' written on it in flowery letters. Slowly Damian reached out to take hold of the doorknob, while making a mental note to wipe off his fingerprints afterwards.

Suddenly the doorbell rang and Damian's hand jerked back from the doorknob as though it were electrified. The sound had been so unexpected in the silence of the empty house that his heart had responded instantly by pounding violently against his chest, causing him to take great gulps of air to stop himself from fainting. The bell rang again, demanding an answer.

Trying to calm himself, Damian ran down the stairs and opened the front door. A short man with a small, bald head and a very large beer gut stood on the doorstep holding a clipboard.

"Delivery for Mr. Crockett," said the man in a rather off-hand manner.

"It's all got to go through the garage and into the back garden," said Damian, cursing the fact that he would now have to try to keep his wretched teddy T shirt clean and wash his hands and feet again before entering Bianca's room.

"Oh no, no, no, no," said the man slowly, sucking in his teeth and shaking his little bald head. "My job is to unload the van. Once I've done that it's up to you where you put the stuff. I've got a bad back, you know."

You've got a bad front as well, thought Damian under his breath, but he kept his cool. Without the van driver's help there was a real possibility Bianca would be back before he could get into her room. "Look," said Damian agreeably, "I can see you like a drink. My dad's just been over to the hypermarket in Calais and come back with some extra strong export lager. If you give me a hand getting the plants and stuff into the back garden, I'll let you have a couple of cans."

"Make it a round half dozen and you've got yourself a deal," said the driver smiling and licking his lips.

How he would explain the loss of his father's prized export lager was something Damian did not like to think about, but this was an emergency. He nodded his agreement and the driver started to unload the van. Once everything was in the front garden Damian was annoyed to realise that he was being left to carry all the heavy bags of fertiliser through to the back garden, while the van driver strolled casually back and forth with the lightest of the plants.

After a few trips Damian's back was hurting and sweat was trickling down his face, making a damp, dirty ring around the neck of the T shirt. Clumps of fertilizer escaped from the bags and smeared the front and the heavy-duty metal staples which closed the tops snagged large threads out of the teddy motif. As he grimly carried the last bag, the driver delicately brought a small fern in a light plastic pot.

"That's yer lot, then," said the driver grinning broadly. "Many hands make light work and all that."

Damian narrowed his eyes and ground his teeth with rage but there was nothing he could do. He stomped into the kitchen and found his dad's stash of beer. Taking four cans he thrust them into the driver's hands.

"'ere, we agreed six," said the man, aggrieved.

"Sorry mate, I thought my dad still had plenty left but he's obviously drunk it all. I'm a bit worried about him, actually. I think he might be a bit of an alcoholic on the quiet. Gets a bit belligerent when he's had a few as well. You should see the black eyes he gives my mum – phew!"

The van driver looked rather nervous at the thought of Mr. Crockett possibly returning to discover his beer had disappeared and backed away from the front door towards the safety of his van. "Yeah, well, I'll be off then."

Damian closed the front door and slumped against it exhausted. But a quick look at the hall clock galvanised him into action again. It was already nearly 6 o'clock and he was extremely dirty and sweaty. Kicking off the old trainers he'd used to go into the garden, he sprinted up the stairs and into the bathroom, pulling off his clothes as he went and leaving them trailing in his wake.

As the first drops of cold water hit his body Damian cursed the fact that his family did not possess a power shower. Hot water took ages to filter through to their old shower head and he could not afford to wait. He shivered as he quickly washed off as much of the grime as he could, wincing as the needles of cold water pricked his skin. Grabbing a clean, white towel he ran across to his bedroom, leaving a trail of wet footprints across the hall.

Once in the safety of his room he rubbed himself all over with the towel, as much to try and warm up as to actually dry his body. When he'd finished the towel was a shadow of its former self – damp, grimy and very sorry for itself. He threw it in the corner on top of his school uniform, not thinking that the wetness would probably seep through to crease and dampen the clothes he would need to wear in the morning.

Damian fumbled through the tangle of clothes which had once been his mother's neat pile of ironing. He found a clean pair of underpants and his football shorts and shirt. At last he was ready for action.

Once again Damian stood outside Bianca's bedroom, reached for the doorknob and turned it. As the door opened he was immediately enveloped in a soft, pink glow. Everything in the room was coloured in varying shades of pink and the overwhelming girliness of it made him want to turn round and leave immediately. Several pairs of hostile, dolly eyes watched him as he started gingerly to look around the room. He unknowingly stepped on a small, woolly lamb lurking just under the bed which let out a loud, mechanical 'Baaaaaaa!' Damian jumped back in shock and sat down heavily on the bed, disturbing the immaculate pink duvet cover. He tried to smooth out the rumples but it just seemed to make things worse. He was muttering under his breath about the obsessive tidiness of females when suddenly he froze.

"Psssssssst!"

Damian paused and looked around, thinking 'nah, it must have been a bluebottle or something'.

"Pssssst!" The sound was louder this time and more insistent.

"Who's that?" said Damian rather nervously.

"Over here." The rather squeaky, child-like voice was coming from the shelf by the window.

Damian went over to peer closely at the dolls and cuddly toys staring back at him. Suddenly the plastic gnome which Bianca had won at the Party Pod stuck out its chubby little hand and Damian nearly jumped out of his skin.

"I'm Plug," said the gnome smiling nervously.

Hesitantly Damian reached out and took hold of the gnome's outstretched hand and shook it. "I'm Damian."

"You've got to help me," Plug went on excitedly. "I saw you had green tears on your clothing at the Party Pod, so I know you must have seen…" At this point he lowered his voice to a whisper and leaned close to Damian's ear. "You must have seen Pling and Plong."

"You're another Kloptronian, aren't you?" said Damian smiling at the thought of more adventures.

"Yes. Pling and Plong are my older brother and sister. I came with them on their mission, but we got separated. Please, where are they? I have to get back home, I can't keep up this gnome disguise much longer."

"How come they didn't mention you?" asked Damian suspiciously.

Plug looked a bit sheepish, staring down at his oversized red plastic shoes, shuffling his foot back and forward with embarrassment. "Well, the thing is… er what happened… um…"

Damian was getting impatient. "Get on with it, my sister will be back soon and there'll be hell to pay if she finds me in here."

Plug stood to attention with fear. "Not that girl child. Keep her away from me. Last night she put her dolls' clothes on me and made me drink imaginary tea from this little cup and saucer – yeuk!"

"Yep, that sounds like Bianca. You'd better talk fast, otherwise I can't begin to describe what she might do to you next time." The air of menace in Damian's voice was enough to loosen Plug's tongue.

"The truth is I stowed away on the space ship. Pling and Plong had told me I was too young to go with them and that I had to stay behind and help mum and dad with all the chores while they were away." Plug looked pleadingly at Damian. "Don't you think that was really unfair? I mean, why should I miss all the fun and adventure and..." Plug's voice trailed away and small globs of green goo appeared in the gnome's eyes. "...now I just want to go home." He sniffed and sighed so loudly, and was obviously so unhappy and scared that Damian was afraid the gnome disguise would disappear completely.

"Look, cheer up, mate. I'll help you get home, don't worry," said Damian, patting the little gnome on the head. "First thing is we've got to get you out of here."

Even as he spoke Damian heard the key turning in the front door. The family were back. He quickly picked up Plug, rearranged the other things on the shelf to fill the gap, and tiptoed out of Bianca's bedroom, closing the door as quietly as possible. Not pausing to wipe off the fingerprints, he crept along the landing to his bedroom and closed the door behind him, breathing heavily with anxiety.

Clutching Plug to his chest and pressing his ear against the bedroom door, Damian could hear Bianca bouncing up the stairs. Her bedroom door opened and then came the scream. "Muuuuuummmmm! Damian's been in my room and the whole place is a mess. Muuuuuummmmm!"

Damian's heart was thumping hard as Mrs. Crockett's footsteps clumped up the stairs. He could hear her pause on the landing and mutter to herself.

"What are these dirty jeans and T shirt doing on the floor? Can't the wretched boy even put his clothes in the laundry basket? I despair, I absolutely despair."

Damian had forgotten that he had carelessly dropped his dirty things in his rush to get into the shower. He also became very conscious of the fact that he was standing in his bedroom in his football kit, holding a plastic gnome – Bianca's plastic gnome. Looking rapidly left and right he tried to decide on the best place to hide Plug. Knowing Bianca, she wouldn't give up until she had checked everywhere – even under the bed where Damian, himself, never dared venture.

Then the open window caught his eye. Of course, he could put Plug on the windowsill and then retrieve him when the fuss had died down. No one would think to look *outside* the room. Plug didn't seem too happy with this idea and started to struggle.

"Don't put me out there, it's cold and dark and…"

Damian put his hand over Plug's mouth and hissed in his ear, "Now look, you'll be all right and it will only be for a few minutes. Now keep still and, for goodness' sake, keep quiet, or we're all in trouble." He put the shivering Plug on the windowsill, closed the window and drew the curtains.

Just then the bedroom door burst open and Bianca stood there looking like a very angry terrier. "How dare you go into my room," she screamed. "I'll have to have clean bedclothes and *everything* now. Who said you could touch my things? I hate you!"

"Now, now, Bianca," soothed Mrs Crockett, "Calm down. I'm sure there's a perfectly simple explanation, isn't there, Damian?" She looked at Damian more in hope than expectation that this time he would, indeed, be innocent.

Damian smiled nervously, "Mum, you know I would never go into Bianca's room unless it was a real emergency." Under his breath he muttered that he couldn't cope with all that sickly pink for a start.

"What was that last bit?" asked his mother, "I didn't quite catch it."

"Oh, er, nothing important." Damian gave her a lopsided grin in the hope of winning her over.

"Well," she said impatiently, "I'm waiting for an explanation." Bianca had lost her manic glare and had now folded her arms smugly; waiting for what she hoped would be such an improbable story that all her parents' recent antagonism would be turned forever from her on to her brother.

Damian swallowed hard, his throat dry with nerves. "Actually, it must have been the delivery man," he began, thinking as he went along. "While I was moving the plants and stuff into the back garden, he asked if he could use our loo. I just told him to go up the stairs and turn left, but he must have turned right and gone into Bianca's room by accident." He tried to direct a concerned look in Bianca's direction. "He didn't steal anything, did he?"

"Of course he didn't," said Mrs. Crockett briskly. "I couldn't see anything out of place in Bianca's room. She's obviously just over-excited after the show."

Bianca was completely wrong-footed by this unexpectedly plausible explanation, opening and closing her mouth while desperately trying to think of something to say.

Mrs Crockett frowned at Bianca. "There you see, it wasn't Damian at all. I think you owe your brother an apology, don't you?"

Bianca went scarlet with embarrassment and rage. Yet again her plans to get Damian into their parents' bad books had gone wrong and she was being forced to say sorry. She squirmed and twisted around in

51

the doorway, trying to bring those loathsome words out of her mouth. "I'm sorry, Damian," she said, so softly that Mrs. Crockett made her repeat them, which added to her embarrassment tenfold.

"That's OK, Bianca. I wouldn't like anyone coming into my room while I wasn't here, either. I'm sorry I didn't keep a better eye on him." Damian was enjoying every moment of her discomfiture and inwardly congratulating himself on his own genius.

"Yes, well, I can't think *anyone* who would want to venture in here without an escort," said Mrs. Crockett sarcastically. "Why can't you tidy up a bit occasionally? And it's like a sauna in here, let's get some air in for goodness' sake." So saying she walked carefully over to the window, stepping cautiously over the many unidentified objects scattered across the floor. Damian drew in his breath sharply as to his horror she then moved one of the curtains slightly, reached through the gap and opened wide with window. He thought he heard a faint cry but the loud thud in the next door garden was unmistakable.

"What was that?" asked Mrs. Crockett.

"Oh, probably the neighbours' cat," stammered Damian.

Just then Mr. Crockett appeared behind Bianca. "What's all the noise up here?" He took one look at his son and raised a quizzical eyebrow. "I didn't realise the school had started arranging football practice in the dark," he said.

Damian blushed, suddenly aware of his skinny, white arms and legs protruding from the baggy shirt and shorts and completely forgetting about Plug. He mumbled something about it being the only thing he could find to wear after taking off his dirty jeans and T shirt. Mrs. Crockett tutted loudly at her son's inability to find anything clean in the black hole of his room but was interrupted by her husband before she could voice her disapproval.

"Son, I have to say you did a great job moving all that stuff into the back garden. For once you've earned your money. Here's a tenner – get yourself a new T shirt. That one on the landing's absolutely had it. It's good to see you put so much effort into something."

Damian grinned broadly. "Thanks, dad. Sorry I left the dirty stuff lying around, mum. I just had to have a shower when I'd finished. I was going to pick everything up and put it in the laundry basket, honest, but you got back before I could get round to it."

"Oh all right," said Mrs. Crockett smiling back at him. "I suppose I am a bit hard on you sometimes." She moved forward to give him a kiss but he stepped quickly to one side so she only caught his ear.

"Leave the lad alone, mother," said Mr. Crockett. "I remember when I was his age being kissed was the pits. But then I met your mother and all that changed." He smiled and winked at Mrs. Crockett who blushed like a little girl.

"Oh stop it, Harold," said Mrs. Crockett smiling up at him. "We'll talk about the old days later, when the kids are in bed," she giggled, digging him playfully in the ribs and winking extravagantly.

Mr. Crockett smiled fondly at her and together they went down the stairs, towing a reluctant Bianca behind them. Damian thought he saw his dad pat his mum's bottom as they went. 'Nah, he said to himself, couldn't have done.' He shook himself to get rid of the unpleasant sight. 'Gross!' he thought.

A faint noise from outside caught his attention. "Heeeelllllppppp!" Plug! Damian ran to the window and looked out into the darkness. He could just see over the neighbours' fence that Plug had landed in the middle of the rockery where Mr. & Mrs. Parker had their very own collection of garden gnomes.

"Plug can you hear me?" said Damian in as loud a whisper as he dared.

"Yes," said Plug in a wobbly voice.

"Are you all right?"

"I landed on some soft, mossy stuff, so nothing's broken. But it's so cold and dark down here and all these other gnomes look really scary, I think they're going to attack me. Please come and get me." Plug sounded desperate.

Damian felt really sorry for the little Kloptronian but he had to be careful. "I'm sorry, Plug, but you'll have to wait a few hours. I can't come and get you until everyone is in bed."

"No, please. I can't wait that long, that big gnome over there is going to hit me with his fishing rod, I know it."

Plug's voice trembled with fear and Damian was worried that his gnome disguise would melt away. "Don't be frightened. The gnomes are made of plastic, they can't hurt you. Try to think of some happy thoughts until I can get to you. I know, have you heard this joke:

*What did one candle say to the other candle?"*

"I don't know," said Plug, rather confused by this change of subject.

*"Let's go out tonight!"*

Damian thought he heard a rather uncertain honking chuckle come from the garden below and decided to try again.

*"Where does a king keep his armies?*

Plug was getting the idea now, "I don't know, where does a king keep his armies?"

*"Up his sleevies!"*

The chuckle became a more pronounced giggle which sounded like a small goose chattering to its friends.

*"Knock, knock!"*

"Who's there?" Plug answered from below.

*"Elsie"*

"Elsie who?"

*"Elsie you in a little while!"*

Damian could hear Plug honking happily and decided it was safe to stop.

"Plug, I'll come and get you as soon as I can. Just keep repeating those jokes to yourself and don't get so excited you start floating in the air. OK?"

"OK, Elsie you later, honk, honk," came the reply.

# CHAPTER FIVE

Eleven year old Cressida Parker was just nodding off to sleep when a rustling noise outside made her sit bolt upright in bed. She listened intently and, after a few moments, the sound came again, accompanied by a hissed grumbling sound. She thought she heard the words 'stupid fence' but she wasn't quite sure.

Without turning on the light Cressida tiptoed to the window and peeked through the curtain. It was dark outside but the street lamp gave enough light so that she could see the front garden fairly clearly. A dark figure was scrabbling about in the bushes just by the rockery. It seemed to be looking for something.

Cressida's first thought was to wake her parents but, just as she was turning away from the window, she heard the voice again, more distinctly this time. "Plug where are you? For goodness sake, this isn't the time for 'hide and seek'" It was Damian from next door. Although Damian had hardly spoken two words to her since she moved in last year, the tortured teenage vowels were unmistakable.

'What on earth is he doing down there?' Cressida thought to herself. 'And who is this Plug?' She had to investigate. Pulling on her dressing gown and slippers, and grabbing a torch, Cressida hurried as quietly as she could down the stairs. Trying to unlock the bolts on the front door without making a noise was difficult and with each squeak and clunk she feared her parents would hear her. But all remained quiet as she opened the door and crept out into the garden.

She edged over to the rockery and switched on the torch.

"'Ere, what's going on? Put that stupid light out!" Damian had jumped out of his skin when the torch went on and now its light blinded his eyes.

"Damian Crockett, what are you doing in our garden in the middle of the night?" Cressida tried to sound confident but she was actually quite nervous.

"Who's there?" said Damian, his voice trembling.

"Cressida Parker," she replied firmly, "and if you don't tell me what's going on, I'm going to wake my mum and dad."

"No, no, don't do that," spluttered Damian. "The thing is, I was, er…" There was a long pause while Damian desperately tried to think of something. "I was, er, *sleepwalking*. Yes, that's it. I was *sleepwalking*. You know, walking about, fast asleep, didn't know where I was, ended up here." He took a deep breath, relieved at having come up with such a good excuse.

"Hmmm, a likely story," said Cressida, unconvinced. "I think you were going to burgle our house."

"No, I wasn't, honestly." Damian looked pleadingly at her.

Cressida knew that there was a mystery here and she was determined to get to the bottom of it. "Well, I think I ought to let my parents decide about that," she said. Of course, she didn't really intend to tell them anything of the kind but she hoped it would be an effective enough threat to get Damian to spill the beans.

It worked. "Please don't do that," begged Damian. "Look, if you promise to keep it a secret, I'll tell you – OK? Only for goodness' sake put that light out first or someone might see and then we'll all be in trouble."

"OK," said Cressida, turning off the torch and moving closer to him, so she could pick up his words more easily.

Just then a little voice piped up from the grass, "Damian, you're standing on me, get off!"

"Who was that?" whispered Cressida in surprise.

Damian sighed, "It's a long story. Is there anywhere quiet we can go?"

"Well, I sometimes sneak down to dad's shed at the bottom of the garden when I want to be by myself."

"OK, lead the way," said Damian, picking up Plug.

Cressida went over to the side gate and led the way through to the back garden. She picked her way carefully down the cobbled path and opened the door of the shed. Once she, Damian and Plug were inside, she shut the door, hung a piece of old sacking over the little window and switched on the torch. She sat herself down on a rickety old dining chair her dad had been promising to repair for the past year and looked at Damian.

She knew that Damian was rather scruffy by nature but the sight of him in a, by now, rather grubby football shirt and shorts, with a large duffel coat over the top and Wellington boots made her giggle.

"Wot you laughing at?" asked Damian feeling embarrassed.

"Oh nothing," answered Cressida, covering her mouth to smother the laughter.

"Good," said Damian dramatically, "'cos this isn't a laughing matter. It's life or death."

"You haven't lost one of your wretched footballs over here, have you?" asked Cressida looking peeved. "My dad is always saying that football is more important than life and death."

"No, it's nothing to do with football, it's about aliens." As he said this, Damian took Plug out of his duffel coat pocket with a flourish and put him on an old milk crate in front of her. Then he squatted down on the floor and waited for Cressida to react with suitable awe. He was soon disappointed.

"That's one of mum's garden gnomes. Damian have you gone mental or something?"

But she nearly fell off the already wobbly chair when the 'gnome' spoke to her. "Actually I'm not anybody's gnome, I'm Plug. Pleased to meet you." As he said this, Plug changed back into his normal alien self and lit up the antenna round his neck in greeting.

\* \* \*

Once Cressida had recovered from the shock, Damian – with Plug interrupting every few words – told her all about how the little alien had been left behind on earth and how important it was for them to try and find a way to get him back home.

Damian didn't really expect any useful suggestions to come from a mere girl, but he was in for a surprise. Cressida's dad had always been a keen astronomer and had passed on his love of the stars to his daughter. He had given her an annual subscription to 'Popular Astronomer' magazine for her birthday and she studied it avidly. She also regularly logged on to the NASA website and kept up with all the latest scientific research.

Cressida tapped her finger against her chin as she always did when she was thinking. "Well, I think the most important thing to do is to try and contact the Kloptronian space ship and get them to turn round and come back here as soon as possible before anyone else finds out Plug is here."

"Great idea," said Damian sarcastically. "And just how do you plan to do that? My mobile phone isn't covered for outer space, is yours?"

"Don't be ridiculous," said Cressida crossly. "Plug, you said that your antenna can work telepathically with other Kloptronians. Is that right?"

"Yes," said Plug uncertainly. "But the signals certainly wouldn't be strong enough to reach into space."

Cressida tapped her chin again. "Then we'll just have to boost the signal so that it can reach," she said, grinning at them as if it would be the easiest thing in the world.

Damian and Plug looked at each other with that look which boys keep solely for the purpose of confirming to each other how stupid girls are. The look that says 'she must be out of her tiny mind'.

Cressida saw it, stuck her hands firmly on her hips and leaned menacingly towards them, sticking out her chin with determination. "Well have you two got a better idea?"

Plug and Damian backed away and pointed at each other, mumbling that it was '*him* not *me*'.

"Boys!" said Cressida with irritation. "What are they like?!"

"OK, OK," said Damian, raising his hands in front of himself defensively. "What do you suggest?"

"Whatever it is, can we do it soon," pleaded Plug. "My energy levels are getting low again."

"Right," said Cressida, taking command. "Firstly, we need to get Plug laughing again. What jokes do you know?"

Damian shrugged his shoulders. "I think I've already told him all the jokes I know," he said. "What about you?"

Cressida thought hard.

*"What is H2O 4?"*

Damian and Plug shook their heads.

*"Drinking of course!"*

Both Damian and Plug looked blank.

Cressida looked surprised. "Don't you get it? $H_2O$ is water and when you add 4 the question becomes what is water for, and the answer is water is for drinking."

There was no reaction from the boys. "Hmm," said Cressida thoughtfully, "This is going to be harder than I thought."

*"Teacher – Name two crustaceans."*

When neither Damian nor Plug even smiled, Cressida became impatient. "You must have got that one? Instead of naming a crustacean – something with a shell, like a crab for instance – Mike says Kings Cross Station and Charing Cross Station. It's perfectly simple."

"Yeah, right," said Damian. "Some of us have better things to do with our time than swallow encyclopaedias."

"I can't help it if you're ignorant," snorted Cressida – and so they started squabbling.

"Stop," wailed Plug. "The way you're grumbling at each other is draining my energy levels even more."

"Sorry," said Damian.

"Sorry," added Cressida. "But you must admit Damian's a bit thick."

Damian gave Cressida such a look that Plug was afraid the argument would begin all over again and a trace of green goo appeared in his eyes.

"Now look what you've done," said Damian, "you've upset him."

Cressida was going to argue that it wasn't her who had caused the upset, but thought of better of it. "We'd better sneak him into my house and find something funny for him to watch on the TV."

"Won't your parents hear us?" asked Damian

"Unlikely," replied Cressida. "Dad's a really heavy sleeper and he snores so much that mum wears ear plugs. I think we'll be OK if we keep the volume down."

"Plug, you'll have to keep the honking down, too," added Damian.

"I'll try," said Plug, "but it's very difficult to control."

* * *

Damian had never been in the Parkers' lounge before and thought it was worryingly tidy compared to his house. There were no toys strewn across the floor, no empty glasses and plates from meals in front of the TV and the newspapers and magazines were placed neatly in the magazine rack by the coffee table. He shuddered at the thought of living in such a clean environment.

"Are you all right?" asked Cressida.

"Oh, er, yeah," said Damian. He felt relieved that Cressida had told him to leave his duffel coat and Wellington boots in the hall. The thought of making even the tiniest mess in this perfect room was too awful to contemplate.

Cressida switched on the TV at the lowest volume possible and started flicking through the channels. All the films seemed to be about wars or violent stories about cops chasing murderers of one kind or another. Naturally, Cressida switched channels quickly when anything to do with sex appeared but the only alternative seemed to be learned documentaries with people talking at each other for long periods of time without stopping.

"Here, let me have a go," said Damian snatching the remote from her.

She was going to say something about 'boys and their toys' but to her amazement, with his fingers flying over the buttons, Damian immediately hit upon a Charlie Chaplin movie. Now, Cressida and Damian were far too sophisticated to find Charlie Chaplin's particular kind of silent, slapstick even remotely funny, but Plug was enchanted.

He started to shake, his antenna whirled around in bright colours, and his three mouths let out the familiar honking sound which gradually grew louder and louder.

"Sssssshhh!" hissed Damian. "You'll wake the whole neighbourhood."

"I'm sorry," giggled Plug, "I can't help it." By now he was also beginning to rise from the sofa and float up to the ceiling.

"Hold him down," cried Damian to Cressida, and together they pulled Plug back on to the sofa and tried to muffle the sound of the honking with a cushion over his mouths.

"Be careful," stuttered Plug in between honks, "you're suffocating me."

"Well, keep quiet then," commanded Damian.

Damian and Cressida tried their best to keep Plug quiet and still during the rest of the film but it was extremely difficult as the little alien wriggled and bobbed like an excited puppy.

As the movie came to a close the final scene involved lots of running about, with people chasing each other for no apparent reason and all the prop furniture getting broken and mess everywhere. While Cressida and Damian thought it was extremely silly, Plug adored it, letting out one enormous honk and bouncing up to the ceiling in one jump.

Just then Cressida heard a bedroom door opening upstairs. "Quick, hide, someone's coming!"

Damian tried to grab Plug from the ceiling but couldn't quite reach.

"Leave him," hissed Cressida. "Plug keep quiet up there and don't move."

Damian just managed to hide behind the curtains in the bay window as the lounge door opened. It was Mrs. Parker. Fortunately, because she had switched on the hall light to come downstairs, she didn't bother to turn on the light in the lounge. All she could see was the flickering TV screen, with Cressida sitting innocently on the sofa.

"Cressida, what on earth are you doing down here at this time? You've got school tomorrow."

Cressida smiled sweetly. "Sorry, mum. I didn't mean to wake you. It's just that there was this special edition of 'The Sky At Night' that I wanted to see."

"Well, why didn't you set the video?"

This logic rather threw Cressida and she had to think quickly. "I, er, would have done, but I couldn't find a blank tape. I didn't want to tape over one of dad's football matches by mistake. You know he never bothers to mark what's on them."

Mrs. Parker nodded. "Yes I do know. He doesn't bother to check what other people have written either. He taped over Auntie Betty's wedding video the other week. I was furious. I'll have to ask her for another copy now and it'll look like we didn't care enough to look after the first one. Wretched man."

So saying, Mrs. Parker turned away to go back up to bed and Cressida was just congratulating herself on averting disaster when her mother suddenly turned round and came back again.

"Why didn't your dad stay up with you? He didn't mention anything about there being an astronomy programme on tonight. You could have watched it together."

Cressida started to fidget and tried not to tap her chin with her finger which would have given away that she was thinking of an appropriate answer. "Um, well, I got the day wrong. I thought the programme was on tonight but it was actually last week. Once I got down here I started watching this Charlie Chaplin film and just got so engrossed I decided to see it through to the end."

Mrs. Parker looked surprised. "You? Charlie Chaplin? Sometimes you amaze me child. Well don't stay up much longer and make sure you switch everything off before you go to bed."

"Yes, mum," said Cressida. She watched her mother carefully to make sure that this time she did go back to bed. Once the bedroom door had closed, Cressida flopped on the sofa with relief.

Damian came out from behind the curtains and they both retrieved Plug from the ceiling.

"I don't think we can risk anymore TV tonight," said Cressida. "You'd better take Plug back to your place."

"I think you're right," answered Damian. "I was trying to peek through the curtains and every time your mum's eyes started to look upwards I was terrified she'd see Plug on the ceiling."

"I know," said Cressida. "Thank goodness she didn't put the light on in here."

"I was worried too, you know," added Plug, sounding a little hurt. "After all, I'm the alien around here. If I get caught, goodness knows what they might do to me." He started to tremble and his antenna drooped.

Damian and Cressida quickly tried to reassure Plug that all would be well. After all the trouble they'd taken to recharge his positive energy, the last thing they needed was for him to get miserable again.

"That Charlie Chaplin's really funny," said Damian. "That time when the others were all chasing him round and round had me in stitches."

"Yes," added Cressida, "and the way he walks and twitches his moustache and twirls his cane. It's really great."

Plug started to perk up as he remembered the film and Damian had to hold him firmly before he floated up to the ceiling again.

Cressida led Damian and Plug back to the front door to let them out.

"Tomorrow I'll go to the library and get a joke book for Plug," whispered Cressida. "And I'll have a think about how we can contact the space ship. Let's meet in the shed at the same time tomorrow night and we'll work out a plan of action."

"OK," said Damian. "I'm sorry, Plug, but you'll have to turn back into a gnome for a while. I'm going to have to put you back into Bianca's room before she notices you're missing."

"Oh no, don't do that, Damian. Not the pink room again."

"I'm afraid so, but it will only be for one day I promise."

As Damian started walking down the path he stopped, seemed to make up his mind about something, and turned round again. "Thanks for your help tonight, Cress. You're really not bad for a girl."

Cressida smiled and waved back at him before she shut the door and turned off the hall light.

# CHAPTER SIX

Damian found it much harder to get to Mr. Parker's shed without Cressida to lead the way. By the time he had safely flopped down on the rickety chair he had several scratches from the rose bushes and a large bruise from banging his shin against the old sink in which Mrs. Parker grew herbs. He took Plug out of his duffel coat pocket and put him on the milk crate so that he could change out of his gnome disguise.

Despite his aches and pains Damian felt extremely pleased with himself. Everything had gone to plan. When he had sneaked back into his bedroom the previous night he had just been wondering how he might get Plug back into Bianca's bedroom when she unknowingly gave him the perfect opportunity. Damian heard her bedroom door open so he opened his own door a crack and peeked out. Bianca walked briskly to her parents' door, dragging her pink teddy bear, and went in without knocking. Damian could just make out the conversation that followed.

"Mum, can I sleep with you?"

"No, dear. Go back to bed before you wake your dad."

"But teddy can't get to sleep and he's keeping me awake."

Mrs. Crockett stifled a large yawn. "Why don't you sing teddy a lullaby, then you'll both get to sleep."

"Will you come and sing us both a lullaby?"

"No, dear. I'm too tired to sing tonight. You have a lovely voice, I'm sure teddy would prefer to hear you sing." Damian could hear his mum pulling the duvet further up round her chin in the hope that Bianca would go away.

"But I'm too wide awake to sing. Teddy will only be able to sleep if we come in with you."

"Oh Bianca." Mrs. Crockett's voice was becoming more despairing.

"Pleeeease, mummy."

Mrs. Crockett admitted defeat. "Very well, dear. But be careful, don't disturb your dad…"

Before she could finish the sentence Bianca bounced on the bed giving the mattress a violent shudder. Mr. Crockett twitched half awake and muttered, "Wassa matter?"

"Nothing, dear," said Mrs. Crockett. "Just go back to sleep."

Damian waited a few minutes to make sure everyone had gone back to sleep and then tiptoed into Bianca's room and put Plug back on the shelf.

"You won't leave me here, will you?" asked Plug anxiously.

"It's just until tomorrow night, I promise. Just keep thinking about Charlie Chaplin and you'll be fine."

Damian tried to blot out of his mind Plug's less than straightforward retrieval from Bianca's bedroom just a few minutes earlier and was so absorbed in doing so that he didn't hear Cressida coming until she actually opened the shed door.

"Hi Damian. Did everything go OK last night?"

"Yep. No probs."

"But we did nearly get caught when you came to get me this evening," interrupted Plug.

"Gosh, what happened?" asked Cressida as she covered the window with the sacking and switched on the torch.

The torch light gave the shed an eerie glow which created exactly the right atmosphere for telling stories about narrow escapes.

"Oh it was nothing, Cress, really," said Damian, trying to make light of it. "I had everything under control."

Plug gave a scornful snorting noise and Cressida raised her eyebrows questioningly.

Damian looked a bit sheepish. "Well, I had hoped that Bianca would go and sleep in mum and dad's bed like she did last night, but

74

somehow she'd managed to knock the alarm clock off the bedside table during the night so they'd all overslept. Mum was rushing about, tutting like a demented squirrel and dad was in a foul mood because he didn't have time to have a proper breakfast and read the paper. They both swore that Bianca would never be allowed to sleep in their bed again. I tried ever so hard to persuade them that it wasn't really her fault but they were absolutely adamant. She was too old to be sleeping in their bed and that was that."

"So what did you do?" asked Cressida.

"I did think about putting one of mum's sleeping tablets in Bianca's hot milk but I thought it might be a bit dangerous. So, in the end, when mum wasn't looking, I put a large slurp of dad's brandy in it."

"Oh Damian, that could have been dangerous as well. Alcohol affects children much more than adults."

Cressida sounded shocked and Damian experienced a completely new emotion. For the first time in his life he cared what a girl thought about him and he was upset by her disapproval. He felt himself blushing and hoped that she wouldn't notice in the torchlight.

Cressida seemed to sense Damian's discomfiture and tried to sooth him. "I'm sorry, Damian. I'm sure I would probably have done exactly the same in your shoes. Did it work?"

Plug coughed and Damian shot him a hard look.

"Not exactly," said Damian. "When I went into Bianca's room after everyone had gone to bed I noticed that the glass of milk on her bedside table was still full. She obviously hadn't liked the taste. She seemed to be asleep anyway, so I went to pick up Plug from the shelf and make my exit."

"But you picked up the wrong thing, didn't you Damian?" said Plug sarcastically.

Damian looked aggrieved. "Well, it was dark and there were lots of things of the shelf. How was I to know Bianca had put that stupid toy lamb up there. Last time I saw it, it was under the bed."

"It made this huge baaing noise," said Plug. "Damian stood frozen to the spot and I thought Bianca was bound to wake up and see him but she just turned over and carried on sleeping."

"I wasn't frozen to the spot, I was thinking what to do," said Damian hotly. "Anyway, I managed to get out with Plug and no damage done."

"Lucky for you," said Cressida sympathetically. "It must have been terrifying."

Plug didn't know what this new mutual appreciation society between Cressida and Damian was all about but he was certain he didn't want it diverting attention from the central problem – how to get him home.

"Can we please forget about Bianca and get on with finding a way to contact Pling and Plong?  My energy is getting low again.  Being in that pink bedroom is very draining."

"Oh, sorry, Plug," said Cressida.  "I went to the library today and borrowed this."  She leaned forward and showed Plug the cover.

"The Biggest Joke Book Ever," he read.  "That's great.  Can I hear a few now?"

"Maybe just one," she said uncertainly.  "We must get on with setting up the equipment."

"Equipment?  What equipment?" asked Damian.

"This equipment," said Cressida, removing with a flourish a faded table cloth covering a box in the corner.  Inside was an old radio, various batteries, a karaoke microphone, some bits of wire and a long roll of cable.

"What on earth are you going to do with that load of old rubbish?" asked Damian scornfully.  Cressida looked crestfallen and he felt suitably guilty.  "Sorry, Cress, I'm sure you've got it all worked out.  It's just that I'm hopeless with electrical stuff.  I wouldn't have a clue where to start."

Cressida smiled at him and Damian felt rather nervous about this strange urge he had to please her and the warm glow that swept over him when he managed it.

"The plan," said Cressida, talking like a school teacher, "is that we connect the radio to the satellite dish on the side of our house using this spare cable for TV aerials and then attach one of Plug's antennas to the radio to send out a signal."

"Will it hurt?" asked Plug uncertainly.

"It shouldn't do," said Cressida confidently. "All the electrical power will be going up to the satellite dish not back to Plug."

"Sounds good to me," said Damian. "How do we get the cable up to the satellite dish?"

"Well, there is a ladder at the back of the house you could climb up, but I'm worried someone might see us," said Cressida.

"Hmmm," muttered Damian, "we need something that can go up the side of a wall without being seen." Suddenly his face lit up. "Got it," he said, snapping his fingers. "A rat!"

"Damian, I don't want to be difficult," said Cressida kindly, "but we don't happen to have any trained rats around here at the moment."

"No," said Damian triumphantly, "but we do have an alien who can change himself into anything he wants."

They looked at Plug expectantly. Plug for his part looked rather uncertain. "You mean you want me to change into a rat, run up the wall of the house, fix the cable to the satellite dish and then come down again?"

"That's about it," said Damian.

"I think I'm going to need a few jokes to be able to do that," Plug said looking worried.

"No sooner said than done," said Cressida picking up the book.

*"How do you know that carrots are good for your eyes?"*

*"Because you never see a rabbit with glasses!"*

*"Where do astronauts leave their spaceships?"*

*"On parking meteors!"*

and so it went on until Plug had to tell them to stop because he was getting light-headed.

* * *

When Plug changed himself into an enormous rat, Cressida had to stop herself from screaming. It was only the little honking sounds that came from his rather fearsome mouth that reassured her. He gripped the length of TV cable in his little pointy teeth and set off across the garden and up the outside of the drainpipe.

Once on a level with the satellite dish, Plug changed his body into that of a small child. He wrapped his legs round the drainpipe and fiddled around with the cable. Down on the ground Cressida and Damian watched nervously as, every time he reached out to work on the dish, he seemed to be in real danger of falling.

Eventually Plug managed to fix the cable and gave them the 'thumbs up'. This caused him to wobble so badly Damian and Cressida had to hold their breath. They were both relieved to see him change back into a rat and begin scuttling back down the drainpipe.

No one noticed the bright green eyes staring silently out from behind the wheelie bin. In a split second a flying ball of ginger hair launched itself towards Plug as he set off across the grass. It was Tibbles, the Parker's tomcat, whose idea of heaven was a large rat to hunt.

Cressida and Damian watched in horror as Tibbles landed just in front of Plug. His ginger fur was standing on end and he snarled menacingly with teeth bared. Damian picked up a spade that had been left by the wall and marched forward to try and chase Tibbles away.

"Don't hurt him," wailed Cressida. "He's a lovely cat really."

"Yeah, lovely," hissed Damian, trying to poke at the cat without actually touching it.

But Tibbles was not going to be denied his prey and he sprang over the spade to land squarely on the rat's back.

"Oh no," cried Cressida, grabbing Damian's arm.

Just then, the rat decided he had had enough of this and suddenly changed into a very large, slobbering rottweiler. Tibbles fell off its muscled back and landed in a heap on the path. The cat backed away hissing and spitting but clearly terrified by this sudden turn of events. Plug let out a low, threatening, growl and Tibbles made a run for it through the fence to the safety of the Crockett's garden.

With the danger over and Plug changed back to his alien form, Cressida realised she was still clutching Damian's arm. She quickly removed her hand as though Damian's skin had suddenly become red hot to the touch and they both seemed embarrassed.

Plug sighed deeply. "Come on you two, we need to get back to the shed and set up the radio."

* * *

Once back inside the shed Cressida connected the TV cable to the radio and hooked it up to the extra batteries. She plugged in the karaoke microphone, opened up the top, exposing the wires inside.

"Now, Plug, I need you to let me attach two of your antenna to these wires here, so that your thoughts can go through when you speak the message."

Plug seemed reluctant to be wired up to the machine, but his desire to get home overcame his nerves. Cressida carefully twisted the antenna around the wires as tightly as she dared without hurting Plug.

"Now, we switch on the radio and see what happens," she said brightly, though she kept her fingers firmly crossed.

Plug screwed up all of his eyes and concentrated as Cressida switched on the radio and started twiddling the dial to see if she could get a signal but there was silence.

"Here, you have a go, Damian. You managed to find Charlie Chaplin without any trouble, see what you can do with alien space ships."

Damian took over and, much to his own surprise, a faint crackling noise came through. Listening intently he thought he heard

*'Why are cooks mean?'*

*'Because they beat the eggs and whip the cream!'*

"It's them," he said excitedly. "It's the comedians."

"Let me listen," said Cressida leaning closer, but the sound faded away.

"Oh no, the signal's not strong enough," said Cressida, close to tears.

For a moment all three of them were silent with disappointment. Then Damian remembered the Kloptronian crystal Pling and Plong used to boost their powers.

"Plug do you have a Kloptronian crystal?"

"Yes, every Kloptronian has one. But mine's only small. They don't let us young ones have the really powerful crystals in case we do something awful with them."

"Let's have a look," said Damian.

Plug pulled out from a pocket in his tummy a small, shiny crystal.

"Plug if you focussed your thoughts through the crystal would it boost their power?"

Plug looked thoughtful. "I suppose so, I've never tried it."

"Well it's time to try it now," said Damian. "It might be our only chance."

"We'd better keep the message short and simple," added Cressida. "We might only have a couple of seconds."

"OK, let's get the space ship to meet us somewhere," said Damian. He grabbed one of Mr. Parker's plant labels and his marker pen in order to write out a short message.

"Plug, how long do you think it would take Pling and Plong to get back here?"

Plug thought for a moment, "I would guess – assuming that they're at full power – about, um, an hour?" He didn't seem too sure but it was the best they had to go on.

"If you say so," said Plug, "but it seems an awful long way to come in an hour."

"Kloptronian space ships are very powerful," Plug went on. "We can cover distances in space that your scientists can only dream about."

"Right then," said Damian scribbling furiously on the plant label, "Here you go, Plug, send this."

Plug started to concentrate on the crystal and it began to glow brightly. Damian worked the radio dial and Cressida kept the joke book ready in case Plug's energy levels started to flag.

Faintly at first the sound of honking laughter filtered out of the radio. Then a strange squeaking and squealing noise came through.

"It's Pling," said Plug excitedly, "He's trying to speak to me."

"Just send him the message," snapped Damian, "We don't have time for conversation." He had noticed that the wires attached to the radio were beginning to melt alarmingly.

Plug closed all his eyes, opened all his mouths and said, "Urgent - Asco's car park, Peckham - midnight, Damian."

Just as the last word was out of his mouths the wires melted completely and the radio went dead.

Everyone went quiet and no one dared to speak. Eventually Cressida broke the silence. "Do you think the message got through?"

"There's only one way to find out," said Damian. "We have to be at Asco's car park in less than an hour. Come on, let's go."

Just then there was a loud crash outside the shed. Damian rushed outside to find Bianca lying in a heap on the ground. She had been standing on a plastic recycling bin watching through a gap in the sacking over the window.

\* \* \*

After Damian had dragged her into the shed and sat her on the rickety chair he glared at her menacingly. "Bianca, what on earth are you doing here?" He was furious.

"Don't you look at me like that Damian Crockett," she said with as much bravado as she could muster. "The real question is what are *you* doing here?"

Damian clenched his fists to suppress his rage but his voice was trembling with anger. "Bianca you are *this* close to getting a slap, so start talking."

Bianca could see Damian meant it so she swallowed hard and began to explain. "Actually, it's all your fault," she began, trying to shift the blame. "If you hadn't come into my room and woken me up I wouldn't be here."

"So you were just pretending to be asleep?" said Damian through gritted teeth.

"Of course I was. No one could sleep with you thundering around the room like a mad elephant.

"Well, why didn't you *say something*," shouted Damian, throwing up his arms in disbelief.

"Keep your voice down," whispered Cressida, "you'll wake the street."

86

Damian turned away, running his fingers through his hair in frustration.

"Why didn't you say something?" asked Cressida more calmly.

"I wanted to know what was going on," said Bianca. "Damian's been so nice to me lately I knew he had to be up to something. So I followed him and that, that – thing." She pointed with horror at Plug.

"I am not a 'thing', I'm a Kloptronian and my name is Plug."

"Well excuse me," said Bianca tartly. "As far as I'm concerned you're a 'thing' and I'm going to tell mummy and daddy about you, so there."

"Now Bianca, try to be reasonable," said Cressida soothingly. "It's very important that we don't tell anyone about Plug. Do you understand?"

"It's no good trying to reason with *her*," interrupted Damian. "The only thing she's concerned about is what's in it for *Miss Bianca Crockett*." Damian squatted down in front of Bianca and put his face as close to hers as he could. "Now listen you, I'm going to make this very simple for you. If you say anything to anyone about this I will personally paint every square foot of your bedroom black – including the window – and, if there's any spare paint left I'll spread it all over that sickly pink carpet of yours."

"Oh Damian, don't say that," said Cressida horrified.

Damian looked up at Cressida. "It's OK Cress, you don't know her like I do."

"You wouldn't dare," snapped Bianca, clearly worried.

"Oh wouldn't I," said Damian menacingly. "Nothing would give me greater pleasure. I might even rip the heads off all those soppy Barbie dolls as well, just for good measure."

Damian knew that Cressida was extremely proud of her collection of Barbies. She had more than anyone else in her class and she wanted to keep it that way. "Oh look," he said in mock surprise, "She's brought one with her. How convenient." As he said this he quickly reached across to Bianca's dressing gown pocket and snatched the doll by the head.

Seeing her brother clutching one of her beloved dolls did the trick. "All right, Damian, I won't say anything. Only leave my dolls alone." Bianca shrank back on the chair and it leaned backwards alarmingly.

"Good. Now we'd better get to Asco's car park," said Damian, putting the doll safely in his duffel coat pocket.

"Wait," said Cressida. "We'd better get the cable down from the satellite dish before anyone sees it."

"Oh no," sighed Plug. "Not the rat again."

"Don't worry," said Cressida. "I'll keep an eye open for Tibbles. I won't let him attack you again. We can drop the radio and stuff in the bin on the way. There's a collection tomorrow, so we won't leave any evidence."

"I'll come with you," added Damian.

"No, you'd better stay here and keep an eye on Bianca," suggested Cressida.

Bianca looked worried. "Don't leave me alone with him. He's dangerous."

"Don't be ridiculous," said Cressida heading to the door with Plug. "Actually, I think he's rather cute." And as she left she gave Damian a huge wink.

# CHAPTER SEVEN

Harry Perkins scratched his head. He was puzzled. He consulted his clipboard and then scratched his head again. He couldn't find anything about a delivery tonight, yet here was the lorry large as life. Of course, during his five years as a security guard at Asco supermarket, it hadn't taken him long to realise that cock-ups at head office were not unusual and that his delivery schedule might bear little resemblance to reality. But what made this delivery stranger than usual was that he hadn't heard the Asco lorry drive into the car park and there was no sign of a driver.

Harry walked round the lorry, aimlessly kicking the tyres as if they might reveal its secrets. He was so absorbed in his own thoughts that he did not notice the three figures moving towards him.

"'Scuse me mister. We found this little girl wandering about." It was Damian and Cressida. They were clutching a reluctant Bianca firmly by the hand.

Harry was startled by their arrival but quickly recovered himself and cleared his throat in order to speak with calm authority. "Now what have we here?" he said. "You found this little girl, you say?" He leaned closer to Bianca. "And what's your name?" he said as if Bianca were a baby.

Before Bianca could speak, Damian patted the pocket of his duffel coat in which Barbie was in mortal danger. "I don't know," she said, turning her big innocent eyes on the security guard.

"Now, now," he said soothingly. "I'm sure a big girl like you knows her own name. Have a good think."

While Damian, Cressida and Bianca were distracting the guard's attention, Plug had gone round to the back of the Asco lorry and opened the doors. As soon as they'd arrived at the car park Plug had realised that the lorry was the space ship. He had sent a telepathic message to Pling and Plong telling them to keep quiet until he could get to them.

While the aliens stayed hidden the lorry, the comedians slipped quietly out of the back and crept up behind the unsuspecting Harry Perkins. They jumped on top of him and started to bundle him towards one of the large recycling bins intended for old clothes. As Harry struggled, Eddie Bernstein grabbed his radio so that he couldn't call for help.

"Quick," said Eddie, "Let's get him inside. Polly, you sit on the lid so he can't get out."

Polly giggled, "You mean I'll be 'guarding the guard'."

"Something like that," laughed Eddie.

* * *

Back at the lorry Pling and Plong were alternating between telling Plug off for stowing away and hugging him with relief that they'd found him. Damian also received his share of hugs, which made him blush with embarrassment. The more so because Cressida was watching.

"Pling, Plong, may I introduce Cress – er Cressida – she helped me contact you. She's really clever with electronics and stuff like that."

Pling and Plong shook Cressida very formally by the hand and, thinking better of it, gave her a big hug as well. "Thank you so much," they said. "You are obviously a very superior human."

It was Cressida's turn to blush, though she was exceedingly pleased to be considered superior. "You're welcome," she said. "It was fun."

Pling turned to Plug with mock annoyance, "Now, young Kloptronian, we'd better get you home before you get into any more trouble."

"I wasn't in any real danger," sniffed Plug confidently. "I could have worked it out for myself. I just let Damian and Cressida help me because they're my friends."

92

"Right," said everyone laughing. "We believe you."

"Can we go home now?" Bianca's whining voice interrupted the jollity.

"And who is this?" asked Plong looking affectionately at what she thought was a sweet little girl.

"That," said Damian, "is my little sister, Bianca. And don't be fooled – she's a monster!"

Plong backed away nervously, not really understanding that Damian wasn't actually referring to a real monster.

"Well," said Pling briskly, "I guess we'd better be on our way."

Everyone fell silent. Green goo appeared in all of Plug's eyes and he gave Damian and Cressida a big hug. "I'm really going to miss you," he said in a quivery, tearful voice.

"We're really going to miss you too," said Damian. Cressida only nodded her agreement because her eyes were starting to fill with tears too.

"Seamus, you'd better collect Polly from the rubbish bin," said Eddie, who was also covering up his sadness by getting everyone moving.

"What about the guard?" asked Seamus.

"Don't worry about him. I think you'll find he's been so terrified by the whole experience he'll stay right where he is until he's sure it's all over."

Eugene, who had been crying ever since they arrived, piped up, "Please can we go, I *hate* goodbyes."

Gus put a reassuring arm round his shoulder. "Don't worry, old girl, I have feeling it won't be long before we see these kids again. They obviously attract trouble like magnets."

"Oh I hope so," said Eddie, sniffing loudly.

Just as they were beginning to clamber into the back of the lorry and having one last round of hugs, Barbara Blagg craned her long neck and squealed in bewilderment. "What on earth is going on over there?" she spluttered.

Everyone turned to look and they were amazed to see the supermarket staff running out of the doors being pursued by what looked like flying hairdryers and electric toasters. As they dodged about in the car park trying to avoid being hit, neat rows of CDs marched across the tarmac like soldiers, closely followed by the latest DVDs.

Even more bizarrely, frozen chickens were having sword fights against legs of lamb, using French bread sticks as weapons. Potatoes were playing football against a team of carrots, with a cabbage for the ball.

"Oh no," shouted Pling, "The ship's power generation units must be affecting all the products.  But I don't understand how?"

"Maybe the ship's sending out some sort of positive energy wave?" suggested Damian.

"I could understand it if it was just the electrical stuff, but why meat and vegetables as well?" asked Eddie in disbelief.

Cressida tapped her chin with her finger.  "Bar codes," she shouted.

"What?" They all cried in unison.

"Bar codes," she repeated.  "All the products have a bar code attached to them.  They must be picking up the signals and energising everything."

"See, I told you she was superior," said Pling admiringly.

"We'd better get out of here before we do any more damage," said Plong anxiously.

As she said this several large cream doughnuts descended on to Gus' face.

"Direct hit," laughed Seamus as he returned with Polly. Gus, however, was not amused.

"Is the security guard all right?" asked Cressida.

"Oh yes," giggled Polly. "Last we saw several bottles of washing-up liquid were trying to squirt him through the opening in the recycling bin."

"What can we do about all these crazy products? Someone might get hurt." asked Damian as some packs of yoghurt flashed by his head and splattered messily on the side of the lorry. He was also worried about what his parents would say when they heard he'd taken Bianca to a supermarket riot.

Pling thought for a moment. "Hopefully, once the ship has gone all the products will stop dancing around."

"Yes, but what about the staff?" asked Cressida.

"I reckon people will just think they've had a mass hallucination or something," answered Damian. "Everyone knows South Londoners are crazy anyway."

"But you're a South Londoner," said Polly surprised.

"Yeah, well, I rest my case," said Damian smiling.

With that Damian and Cressida closed the doors of the lorry behind Pling, Plong, Plug and the comedians. The large Asco symbol on the side began to shimmer and dissolve until the lorry was completely gone.

* * *

Damian, Cressida and Bianca hid by the car park fence and watched in amazement as all the products dropped lifelessly to the ground. As they were about to leave they noticed a line of black transit vans with a dark limousine in the front drive slowly and very quietly through the gates.

Out of the limo stepped a tall figure in an expensive-looking dark suit. He was wearing wraparound sunglasses even thought it was night time and had an earpiece with a microphone attached into which he was talking urgently.

From two of the vans scrambled a team of people in black boiler-suits and baseball caps. They too had earpieces and they carried strange, futuristic-looking machine-guns. They were clearly military – but from where? The soldiers began to round up the dazed staff from the nightshift and gather them together in the entrance of the supermarket.

Damian, Cressida and Bianca looked on nervously as from the third van came a group of men and women in white coats and carrying medical bags. Each member of the supermarket's staff was given an injection which seemed to make them fall asleep immediately. And, as soon as they were unconscious, the soldiers placed them carefully back in the positions they were working in before the space ship arrived. Even Harry Perkins was put back in his security box by the gate, together with the radio Eddie had left by the rubbish bin.

"What are they doing?" whispered Cressida to Damian.

"Haven't a clue," he answered.

"I don't suppose anyone's interested in my opinion," piped up Bianca, "but I reckon they're clearing up. You know, like in the movies, so no one knows we've been invaded by aliens who are going to exterminate us all."

"Shut up, Bianca," snapped Damian. "We haven't been invaded by aliens and no one's going to be exterminated. They've just paid us a little visit, that's all."

"Bianca could be right, though," said Cressida. "The soldiers are certainly picking up every CD and carrot very carefully and taking them back in the store. They even seem to have replacements for some things – like the cream cakes and the bread."

"Well, whatever they're doing, I think we'd better get out of here before we're seen," said Damian. "I don't know who these people are but I certainly don't want to mess with them."

"I think you're right," said Cressida anxiously. "No one must ever know we've been here."

Instinctively they both turned to Bianca. "No one! Do you understand?"

She smiled weakly but underneath she was already plotting her revenge. Somehow she had to retrieve her Barbie from Damian's pocket before morning. As for the rest of Damian's threats, Bianca figured that, once her parents knew the whole story, he wouldn't be able to touch her things. She could say whatever she liked.

# CHAPTER EIGHT

Damian woke to hear Bianca shouting at the top of her voice, "Mum, dad, Damian's been meeting aliens and he threatened to break my dolls if I said anything."

After saying good night to Cressida, he had made Bianca go back to bed and then crashed out himself. He now looked at the clock and saw that it was after 8.30. 'Oh no,' he thought, 'Bianca must have woken up before me.'

He scrambled out of bed and rushed over to the duffel coat he had thrown down by the door. The Barbie was missing and the door was slightly open. Bianca must have sneaked in and taken it while he was still asleep. Damian clutched his head with his hands and groaned. What on earth was he going to do? Then he heard his mother's voice floating up the stairs.

"Damian, would you come down here, please?"

He had to have time to think. "Just a minute, mum, I'm not dressed."

"Never mind about that. Put your dressing gown on and come down now." Her tone was adamant and Damian knew he would have to go down and face the music.

He pulled on his dressing gown and reluctantly slouched barefoot down the stairs.

"Damian," said Mrs. Crockett. "Bianca has had a rather nasty dream and I'd like you reassure her that you have not been chasing aliens all night."

"But it's not a dream," screamed Bianca. "It really happened."

"Keep quiet, Bianca," insisted Mrs. Crockett. "Now Damian, tell Bianca what you were doing last night."

Damian felt as if a huge weight had been lifted from his shoulders and he wanted to jump around, clapping has hands for joy. He even felt like giving his mum a big, sloppy kiss – but instantly thought better of it. Instead, he kept a very straight face and tried to sound as serious and concerned as possible.

"Well, after I'd gone up to bed I listened to some 'Scar Tissue' on my sound system for a while…"

Bianca interrupted, "So why didn't we hear it? You usually have it so loud your alien friends could hear it in space."

"Now that's enough," snapped Mr. Crockett.

"It's OK, dad," smiled Damian. "If you really want to know, I used the new headphones you bought me for my birthday."

Bianca looked daggers at her brother but he just smiled sweetly back at her.

"After that I went to bed and, unless I've started sleepwalking, I stayed there until you just woke me up – Oh I may have gone to the loo in the night but that's about all." Damian smiled in triumph, his victory over Bianca complete.

"But I can show you the radio they used, it's in the Parkers' dustbin. And the fight at the supermarket is bound to be on the news."

"For goodness' sake, Bianca," shouted Mrs. Crockett, "There's nothing in the dustbin, it's already been emptied this morning."

"And there was absolutely nothing on the news about any alien visitations at our local supermarket – unless you count the so-called chicken in their pies!" added Mr. Crockett smiling to himself for being so smart, so early in the morning.

"Now both of you go and get ready for school, and let's have no more silly talk about aliens." Mrs. Crockett's word was final and Bianca sloped away with the biggest pout on her lips that Damian had ever seen.

\* \* \*

Parked outside the Crockett's house was an electricity company transit van. A couple of men in overalls were pretending to work on a junction box in the road. Inside the van Edward Millichamp was listening to the conversation in the Crockett's kitchen. He flicked a crumb of Eccles cake from his otherwise immaculate suit.

"So, they don't believe her," he said to the man in the white coat who was monitoring the heart rate and blood pressure of everyone in the house.

"Seems not. I've checked everyone's life signs, they're definitely all human. Next door as well."

"Pity," said Millichamp, forming a little bridge with his fingers and pondering what to do next.

"Jenkins, I assume everything was arranged satisfactorily at the supermarket?"

The man in the white coat replied, "Yes, the amnesia drug worked like a charm. Everyone woke up thinking they'd just dozed off for a couple of minutes. Altering the clocks was a masterstroke."

"Thank you, Jenkins. I thought so."

"The Minister isn't going to be very pleased that we've let the aliens slip through our fingers again," said Jenkins anxiously.

"Don't worry, I can handle him." Millichamp was confident of his hold over the government minister in charge of extraterrestrial activity. Having convinced the Prime Minister to spend a billion pounds from the UK budget on setting up a Covert Alien Surveillance Team – CAST for short – there was no way he was going to report anything but success. Millichamp merely had to couch last night's incident in such a way that the minister was made to look good. After that he could get on with the job of finding any and all extraterrestrials without hindrance.

"What do we do next?" asked Jenkins. "The aliens have gone."

"They'll be back," said Edward Millichamp thoughtfully, leaning back in his chair. "They'll be back."

www.ingramcontent.com/pod-product-compliance
Lightning Source LLC
Chambersburg PA
CBHW031846170626
46807CB00004B/1651